CHOCOLATE CHIRP COOKIES

Jenny Goebel

illustrated by

Angie Alape & Marc Monés Cera

Albert Whitman & Company
Chicago, Illinois

William loved to visit the Butterfly Pavilion with his dad and sister. The Exploration Station was his favorite part because there was always something new.

The sign for today read *Entomophagy*. William had no idea what "entomophagy" meant. It sounded very scientific, though, and William liked science. Then he read the rest of the sign: *Featuring a Bug Buffet!*

That couldn't be right. Food was served at a buffet. But bugs weren't food, were they? "Do people eat bugs?" William asked.

"Yes," Dad said. "Many people all over the world eat them every day."

"Really?" William couldn't believe it.

"It's not as common here, but it may be in the future," Dad explained. "Some of the foods we usually eat might become harder to find. Insects can be easily produced without damaging the environment."

Harper's face lit up. "I want to try the Bug Buffet!"

William's face turned a light shade of green. Dad took one look at him and said, "Maybe we should save that for last."

Searching for insects at the first exhibit took William's mind off the idea of eating bugs. The Madagascar hissing cockroaches were easy to find because they made a sound like the rattle of tiny maracas. Suddenly, William's thoughts went right back to eating bugs. He wondered if the cockroaches would be crunchy like potato chips, and that made him queasy.

William found Harper waiting to hold Rosie, a Chilean rose hair tarantula the size of William's palm. Rosie's hairy legs and furry body had always been too much for William. But compared to eating bugs, touching the giant spider didn't seem so bad.

Still, William didn't mind when Harper announced, "I'll go first!"
When it was his turn, William held his breath and stayed as still as
a leaf bug. As Rosie crawled across the back of his hand, her fuzzy
legs tickled him with their light, feathery touch. William smiled. He
was proud of himself.

The next exhibit was Water's Edge. William went straight to the aquarium. Hiding in the gravelly bottom was a mantis shrimp. It had buggy eyes, a flexible shell like a Madagascar hissing cockroach, and bendy legs like Rosie.

At first, William had been surprised to find ocean creatures at a bug zoo. Now he knew that crabs, shrimp, lobsters, spiders, centipedes, and insects were all related. In fact, a friendly zoologist had told him that these creatures were basically cousins.

The next exhibit had hundreds of brightly colored butterflies fluttering all around. William watched the blue morpho butterfly as it drank nectar with its straw-like tongue.

William thought he might like to try nectar, but he still didn't want to eat insects. He swallowed a lump in his throat as Harper tugged him toward the Exploration Station.

The guest speaker greeted them. "How many of you have eaten a bug before?"

Dad raised his hand. "I tried a fried silkworm in Thailand," he said. "It tasted a bit like mashed potatoes with a crunchy layer on the outside."

William's eyes grew as round as a mantis shrimp's. Harper giggled and said, "Ewww!"

A woman nearby said, "My family eats tacos with chapulines—cooked grasshoppers."

"That's great!" the speaker said. "*Entomophagy* is just a fancy word for eating insects. For most people—around 80 percent of the world's population—bugs are part of a regular diet. In fact, eating insects can improve your health and help save the planet."

Dad smiled at William. "What did I tell you?"

William grimaced. Saving the planet sounded good, and he liked bugs, but he still did not want to eat them.

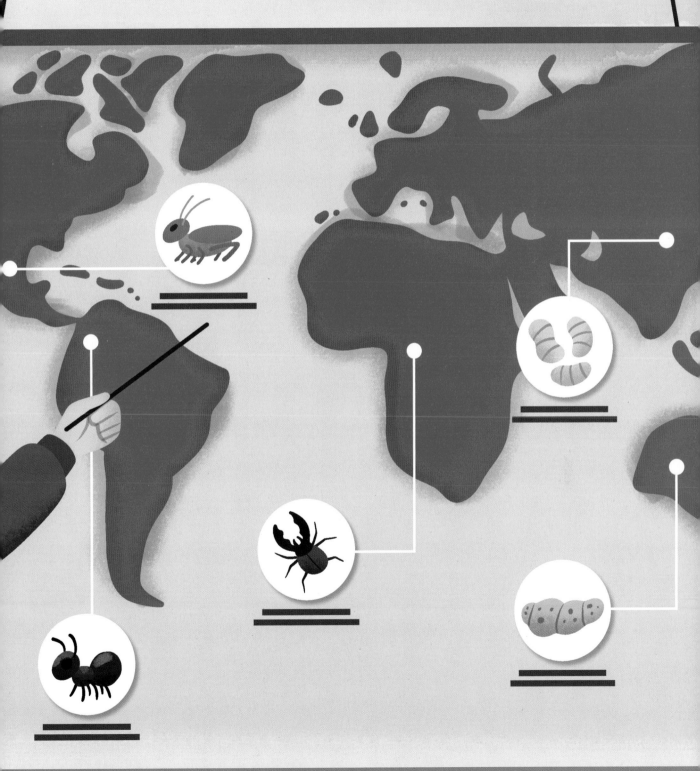

"Raising crickets creates less pollution than raising livestock," the speaker continued. "Not to mention, bugs are an excellent source of protein. They can taste nutty, salty, sweet, or savory."

Just the thought of eating bugs made William feel like Rosie was crawling around *inside* his stomach. He felt even worse when the speaker lifted lids to reveal the Bug Buffet: chocolate-covered larvae, fried waxworms tossed in cinnamon and sugar, and chile-lime roasted grasshoppers.

Harper went straight for the chocolate-covered larvae.
"They taste kind of like chocolate-covered popcorn," she said.
His dad munched on a grasshopper. "Not bad."

When it was William's turn, he froze. "I can't," he croaked.

The speaker nodded. "I understand. It can be hard to get past the yuck factor. Insects are funny looking. But they aren't that different from foods you may already eat, like shrimp and lobster."

William nodded. "I know," he said. "They're related."
Even so, he could not find the courage to eat a bug.
Then he saw the cookies.

"Would you like to try a chocolate chirp cookie?" the speaker asked. "Crickets are ground into powder, and the cricket flour is used to make the cookie dough."

William inspected the cookie. There were no antennae, wings, or thoraxes peeking out from under the chocolate chips. He could not see the crickets, but his stomach still felt full of creepy-crawly things. "I don't know..." he said.

"You didn't want to hold Rosie before today," Dad reminded him.
"But aren't you glad you did?"

William *was* glad. Holding Rosie wasn't as scary as he thought it would be. Maybe eating the chocolate chirp cookie wouldn't be as bad as he thought either.

He took a tiny nibble, and it tasted like...

A regular chocolate chip cookie!
"How about a waxworm now?" the speaker asked.

"No thanks," William said. He wasn't ready to try *all* the insects at the Bug Buffet. William smiled as he polished off the last bite of cookie. He was proud of himself. "If eating bugs is called entomophagy, does this make me an entomophagist?"

"You bet it does," Dad said.

"In that case," William said, "can I have another chocolate chirp cookie?"

To everyone who has ever felt uncomfortable trying something new—JG

To my family, for all the meals we have enjoyed together—AA

To my whole family...and to all the bugs in our garden—MMC

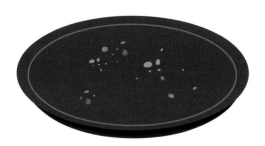

Library of Congress Cataloging-in-Publication data
is on file with the publisher.
Text copyright © 2022 by Jenny Goebel
Illustrations copyright © 2022 by Albert Whitman & Company
Illustrations by Angie Alape and Marc Monés Cera
First published in the United States of America in 2022
by Albert Whitman & Company
ISBN 978-0-8075-1143-5 (hardcover)
ISBN 978-0-8075-1155-8 (ebook)

Printed in China

10 9 8 7 6 5 4 3 2 1 WKT 26 25 24 23 22

Design by Tim Palin Creative

For more information about Albert Whitman & Company,
visit our website at www.albertwhitman.com.